THE NAUGHTIEST UNICORN

IN A WINTER WONDERLAND

PIP BIRD

ILLUSTRATED BY DAVID O'CONNELL

Contents

CHAPTER ONE
Ice is nice!

Mira took a deep breath and pushed out on
to the ice rink in her ice-skates. The little
puffs of steam coming out of her mouth made
her smile as they rose up into the air. Unicorn
School looked completely magical in the winter.
Everything as far as Mira could see was covered
in soft white snow with sparkling icicles hanging
from the roofs and fences.

Mira had only been ice-skating once before,
when her sister Rani had her birthday at the ice
rink. After a while she'd been able to let go of

the rail and skate into the middle of the rink and she'd only fallen over a couple of times.

But now Mira was having to skate carrying a unicorn, which was seriously throwing her off balance.

'Dave,' Mira said, '*please* will you try skating?'

Dave burped loudly and shook his head. Everyone at Unicorn School had a UBFF (Unicorn Best Friend Forever) and Dave was Mira's. He wasn't like the other unicorns, who right now were pirouetting around on the ice, doing synchronised dance moves and generally being very sparkly and elegant. Dave liked doughnuts, naps and doing giant poos – in that order. And he sometimes (quite often) got Mira

into trouble. But Mira loved her UBFF to bits.
They had the best adventures and she wouldn't
change him for the world. (Unless there was
another unicorn who wouldn't refuse to skate.)

Mira was sure that Dave just needed a bit of
encouragement and he'd soon discover his love
for ice-skating. Well, she wasn't *totally* sure, but
her arms were getting a bit tired from carrying
him. So she gently dropped him onto the ice.

Dave's eyes went wide in surprise. His short
legs flailed around and his skates sent swooshes
of ice up into the air. The little unicorn spun
around a few times and landed with a thud on
his bum. He looked up at Mira crossly.

'Great ice-dancing, Dave!' called Fleur from

Class Yellow. Fleur and her unicorn, Sunrise,
were in the middle of performing the whole
of *Frozen 2: On Ice*.

Dave farted in reply. Then he curled up on
the ice and went to sleep. Mira skated in circles
around him, practising her turns. At least he'd
had a go!

Soon Mira heard Miss Hind blowing her whistle to signal the end of After-School Winter Club. Next to Miss Hind was Miss Ponytail, the art teacher, who looked very cold.

'SLOWLY AND CAREFULLY!' yelled Miss Hind, casually spinning on the ice on one skate.

Mira slowly and carefully skated up to the rest of her classmates, who were watching Miss Hind demonstrate a backwards glide. Children from Snowman Club were coming through the snowy paddock, all slipping around in their snow boots and some sliding on their bums. Raheem and his unicorn Brave came bounding over, clutching bags of icicles.

There were lots of wintery after-school clubs to choose from at Unicorn School. Mira had picked ice-dancing, her best friend Raheem had chosen Icicle Studies and their other best friend Darcy had gone for Sledge Hockey Club.

'I've got SO many icicle facts to tell you –' Raheem started to say.

'CALM, please!' said Miss Hind. 'I won't have any snow silliness. Miss Ponytail has some exciting news for you, apparently.'

Whispers went around the crowd as they all wondered what the exciting news was.

Mira couldn't wait to find out. She hopped up and down in excitement, forgetting she was still on the ice rink, and slid sideways into Freya.

Freya immediately fell over.

'Sorry!' Mira whispered as she helped Freya up. Miss Hind gave them a glare.

Miss Ponytail stepped carefully off the ice and on to the snow. 'Gosh, it is chilly out here,' she said.

'What did I miss?' Darcy yelled, zipping across the ice in a sledge and spinning around sideways with a great SWOOSH. Her unicorn, Star, skated close behind.

The ice spray from Darcy's sledge covered Miss Ponytail and Miss Hind, as well as a few members of Ice-Dancing Club.

'Gah pthh pah flmmm gah,' Miss Hind spluttered, spitting the ice spray out of her

mouth. 'That was . . . spectacular, Darcy
and Star. Have you thought of a career in
synchronised skating?'

'I don't think I'm ready to retire from
sledge hockey yet,' said Darcy, spinning her
hockey stick in her hand.

'Isn't sledge hockey terribly violent?' said
Miss Ponytail.

'Yeah!' said Darcy. 'It was so much fun we played extra time AND danger penalties, which is a cool new thing I made up. Sorry, that's why we're late.'

The other children who'd chosen Sledge Hockey Club skated up behind Darcy, looking a bit shaken.

'Are we all here?' said Miss Hind.

The children looked around. Mira hoped the teachers would hurry up and tell them the exciting news!

'Right,' said Miss Ponytail. 'The exciting news is . . .'

'Miss,' said Fleur, putting up her hand, 'Samir's in Snow Cone Club and he's not here.'

Just then, children from Snow Cone Club emerged from school. Tamsin from Mira's class waved and held up her snow cone. 'Mine's strawberry!' she said happily.

'Uh oh . . .' said Mira, looking from Tamsin to Dave.

But it was too late. Dave took one sniff of the strawberry ice cream, jumped up and then

barrelled across the ice as fast as his little legs
would carry him. Unicorns and children dived
out of the way. The Snow Cone Club dropped
their ice creams and ran back to the stables for
safety.

Dave did a double tuck somersault off the
ice and over the barrier, and landed cleanly
right in the middle of all the snow cones. He
immediately ate them all.

CHAPTER TWO
The Winter Expedition

Mira gave Dave a scratch behind the ears.
She had been right that all he needed was a
bit of encouragement to discover his love for
ice-skating! Well, encouragement and ice cream.
And she was sure that Miss Hind had been
impressed, even though she had called Dave
'Danger On Ice'.

'Now, I'm sure you know about the Unicorn
School Winter Expedition,' said Miss Ponytail
with a smile.

Lots of the children in the other classes were nodding. Mira's class gave each other excited looks. Class Red hadn't been on the Winter Expedition before!

'Every year the whole school takes a trip to the Unicorn School Winter Cabin in the Crystal Mountains,' said Miss Ponytail, 'where there are many more lovely, chilly activities to do.'

Darcy put her hand up. 'Will there be sledging?' she said.

'There will be many activities,' said Miss Hind.

'We just want to sledge,' said Tom from Class Orange.

Mira squeezed her hands together in excitement. She hoped they would get to do sledging!

'But this time,' continued Miss Ponytail, 'the Winter Expedition will coincide with a very special and rare event: the Aurora Lights!'

'Ooooooh,' said the children. Mira joined in, even though she wasn't totally sure what the Aurora Lights were.

'Can anyone tell me what the Aurora Lights are?' said Miss Ponytail.

Flo put up her hand. 'Is it when a massive

alien comes down and shoots rainbow lasers out of its bum?'

'I heard they are caused by all the rainbows dancing together,' said Tamsin.

Jake from Mira's class tutted. 'No, it's when a star EXPLODES and the gas eats up all the other planets in the universe.'

'And bum lasers,' said Flo.

'Good guesses!' said Miss Ponytail,

encouragingly. 'It's when the rainbow lights to the north of us create a truly magical display in the sky.'

Raheem cleared his throat. 'They're actually caused by a solar wind passing through a magnetic field in the atmosphere and particles –'

'I've heard it only happens every seventy million years,' interrupted Sarah from Class Blue, nodding wisely.

'Almost!' said Miss Ponytail. 'It's every three years.'

'Will we be able to fly up into the sky and slide down the rainbows?' said Tamsin.

Miss Ponytail thought for a moment. 'No,' she said.

The children groaned.

'But you will be able to watch from a nearby mountain!' Miss Ponytail continued. 'And that brings me to the truly exciting news. This wonderful event has a special quest: the Unicorn School Art Project!'

This time the children cheered. It wasn't quite as good as sliding down rainbows, but it still sounded pretty cool. Miss Ponytail explained that everyone would create a piece of art inspired by the Aurora Lights, using whatever they wanted from the Unicorn School Art Bus. Then they would bring them back to make a display on the big wall by the stables.

17

Everyone headed back to the school. The children stamped their snow boots on the mat outside and the unicorns stamped their hooves. The children shook out the snow from their coats and the unicorns shook out their manes, sending icy flurries everywhere.

Mira's fingers were tingling in her gloves as they started to warm up. But she had an excited tingly feeling all over too. Mira loved Art. Spending the day doing her favourite subject AND sledging with her UBFF sounded like the best quest ever!

She gave Dave a squeeze, and he burped, as he was just finishing the last snow cone.

Later on, Class Red were all snuggled up in their bunk beds in the dorm, too excited to sleep.

Miss Glitterhorn came round and told them to get plenty of rest, as they would be setting off very early in the morning. She turned off the lights and went off down the corridor.

Everyone waited for a minute, then flicked on their torches.

'What's everyone going to do for their art project?' said Seb. 'I'm going to use neon, glow-in-the-dark spray paints.'

'I'm going to knit a rainbow,' said Tamsin.

'I'm going to make a sculpture out of slime and decorate it with my own hair,' said Flo.

'I'll just take a picture on my phone,' said Darcy.

Jake rolled his eyes. 'You can't do that – it's not art,' he said.

Darcy shrugged. 'More time for sledging!' she said and she and Star did a hoof five (which is just like a high five, except one of you has a hoof).

At that moment, Dave did the world's most enormous sleep-fart and made them all jump – and then they all laughed.

'Yay for art and sledging!' cheered Mira.

The rest of Class Red cheered too. They all started chanting, 'ART AND SLEDGING!'

'Art and sledging and SCARY SNOW BEASTS,' said a voice from the door.

Class Red jumped again. Dave did another sleep-fart.

Standing there was Mira's big sister Rani and her friend Lois.

'How come you're not in bed?' said Mira, shining her torch over at her sister.

'We haven't finished packing yet,' said Rani.

Mira saw that Rani and Lois were dragging a giant sack between them. 'What are you taking?' she asked.

Rani and Lois dragged the sack into the middle of Class Red's dorm. Class Red and their unicorns crept forward to shine their torches inside the sack. They saw a jumble of bottles and boxes of various sizes, crystals, rainbow-coloured feathers and drums.

Rani grabbed Mira's torch and shone it slowly round the faces of Class Red. 'Out in the mountains, something dangerous lives,' she whispered.

Brave whimpered and dived under Raheem's bed covers.

Lois took the torch from Rani. 'That's right,' she said, waving the light around. 'Ginormous Snow Beasts. Who like to eat small children!'

There was a silence.

'So . . . you're taking jewellery for them?' asked Darcy, one eyebrow raised high.

Rani tutted. 'No, duh. These are our Important Snow Beast Fighting Tools. They scare off Snow Beasts!'

'How do you know they work?' asked Freya.

'Well, we've been on two Winter Expeditions and both times we took all our Snow Beast Charms and both times we didn't see any Snow Beasts!' said Lois.

'Could it be that you didn't see any because
the Snow Beasts aren't real?' said Mira.

'No, you idiot,' said Rani. 'Look – this is
an amber amulet. It scares off giant ice snakes.'
She held up an orange coloured stone.

'How?' asked Raheem.

'They can smell it,' said Lois. She held up a
wooden stick next, with little holes in it. 'And
this frightening flute makes the exact sound that
forces the dreaded snow squirrel-scorpion to run
away and then burst into flames.'

Lois took out the rest of the Snow Beast
Fighting Tools one by one from the bag and
passed them round Class Red.

Eventually they heard Miss Glitterhorn patrolling the corridor again so Rani and Lois quickly packed up their sack and dragged it towards the door.

'See you at the Snow Cabin . . . if the Snow Beasts don't get you first,' said Rani, giggling as she and Lois left for the Class Yellow dorm.

Mira gave Dave a cuddle and he responded with the loudest sleep-fart yet. She didn't really believe in the Snow Beasts, but she definitely didn't want to meet any of them. She snuggled down under her covers, feeling a bit anxious.

What exactly WAS waiting for them on the other side of the mountains?

CHAPTER THREE
Follow the Stars . . .

Mira stomped her feet in the cold stableyard to keep warm. It was so early that it was still dark and she could see puffs of breath steaming into the cold morning air. The stableyard was packed with unicorns and pupils and their expedition rucksacks. Teachers ran about, checking things off their Expedition Checklists.

Miss Hind and Miss Glitterhorn had already set off in the Unicorn School Art Bus, looking very warm. When Darcy asked why they

couldn't all get a lift in the bus, Miss Ponytail
said that not everyone would fit – and they
would miss out on navigating their own way to
the Snow Cabins by following the stars. Darcy
tried to call the bus back just to take her and
Star, but it was too far away.

Miss Ponytail put them all into mixed class
groups, with a Class Violet pupil to help them

with the navigating. The Class Violet pupil also looked after the star map, because they were the oldest and, Miss Ponytail said, the most sensible. Mira's group were with Yasmin.

'Is that – a unicorn?' asked Mira, pointing to one starry shape on the map.

'Yeah, maybe. But why does it have a spike coming out of its bum?' said Yasmin.

'I think you're holding it upside down,' said Lois.

'That constellation is the Great Unicorn in the Sky!' said Raheem with excitement, pointing upwards to where Mira could just make out the stars twinkling in the same pattern as on the star map. Yasmin said Raheem could look after the map if he wanted to, so he happily took it and jumped on to Brave.

Soon everyone was sitting on their unicorns, and the whole school set off on the trek to the Crystal Mountains. Raheem and Brave were riding at the front of their little group, making sure they were all heading in the direction of the Great Unicorn in the Sky. Mira loved the crunching sound of the snow under the unicorns' hooves.

Tom from Class Orange told Darcy that right next to the Snow Cabins was the best slope EVER for sledging. And Tom's best friend, who was also called Tom, said that when he had sledged down it last year, his sledge had actually flown up into the air.

Mira was at the back as usual. Dave was shorter than the other unicorns, so sometimes he was a bit slower. He also kept stopping to eat snowberries.

They halted at the foot of the Crystal Mountains so the unicorns could have a rest.

'We have to check the area for Snow Beasts!' said Rani. She and Lois trotted around the edges of the snowy hilltop on their unicorns, waving their Snow Beast Fighting Tools in the air and chanting, before eventually sitting down with the others.

'Do you have the special honey for melting the Many-Headed Snow Pigeons, Lois?' said Rani.

Lois nodded, patting the sack of amulets. Dave looked up in interest at the mention of honey, so Mira quickly distracted him with some crisps she'd brought for him.

Most of the unicorns were doing snow angels rather than resting. Dave curled up behind Mira for a quick nap. It was getting lighter now and clouds glowed softly with pinks and purples, though Mira could still see the stars. Every so often a feather floated past her in the air, which

Mira thought was strange as she couldn't see any birds around.

'That's mine!' said Rani, snatching up a feather that had landed on Mira's leg.

'We need them to waft away Snow Butterflies,' said Lois.

'Snow Butterflies don't sound scary!' said Jake with an unimpressed look.

'Yeah, they aren't that bad,' said Lois. 'Until they land on you and suck your brain out of your ear.'

Jake scoffed, but he did pull his hat down further over his ears.

'It's not the scariest Snow Beast though,' said Rani.

'What's the scariest one?' said Mira.

Rani rolled her eyes. 'The Abominable Snowman, obviously!'

'What's abominable?' said Mira.

'Um . . .' said Rani. 'It means . . . er . . .'

'Proper scary,' said Lois.

'Yeah, proper scary,' Rani agreed.

'I thought yetis were the scariest,' said Tamsin.

'The Abominable Snowman *is* a yeti,' explained Lois. 'It's the scariest yeti there is.'

Mira shivered – mostly because of the snow, but a little bit because of the talk about beasts. She was about to ask why the Abominable Snowman was so scary, but Jake interrupted.

'I'm not scared of ANY Snow Beasts,' he said.

'I WANT to meet one.'

'You don't want to meet the Bearded Ice
Warlock,' said Lois. 'He turns your head to snow
with just one glance.'

'What do you have to scare him off, then?'
said Jake.

'This tin of teeth,' said Lois, rattling it.

Miss Ponytail announced that rest time was
over and it was time to start climbing up the
Crystal Mountain. Slowly the unicorns got up
and shook off the snow.

'Are you excited about the Snow Cabins,
Dave?' said Mira, turning round. 'I think there's
going to be hot choc–'

She stopped. Dave wasn't there. There was a

just a Dave-shaped dip in the snow where he'd been having his nap.

'Wh–wh–what's that?' said Tamsin. She was pointing at Rani and Lois's sack, which was starting to move . . .

Jake grabbed a feather and started wafting it furiously. Rani blew frantically into her beast flute and Mira put her hands over her ears because it was possibly the worst sound she'd ever heard.

Out of the sack burst a small, plump shape with a big feathery beard.

Lois leaped in front of everyone. She shook her tin of teeth at the figure, yelling, 'Get back, Bearded Ice Warlock!'

The Bearded Ice Warlock burped in surprise.

'Stop!' yelled Mira, running forward. 'That's not a warlock. That's Dave.'

Rani gave another sharp toot on the flute as Mira reached the sack. Sure enough, her UBFF was peeping out. For some reason, he had feathers stuck all round his mouth.

Jake stopped waving his feather. 'Obviously I knew it was Dave,' he said.

Mira saw that there was an empty jar by Dave's feet. 'I think he might have eaten your honey,' she said to Rani and Lois.

Dave burped again and dislodged two feathers from his beard.

'Well,' said Rani, picking up the jar crossly and putting it back in the sack. 'If we do meet a Many-Headed Snow Pigeon and we all get evaporated, I am blaming YOU.'

∪∪∪

The last bit of the journey was definitely the best bit, as they got into a cable car to go up into the Crystal Mountains. Mira could see for miles. Spread out beneath them were hills and fields of snow, and the school was a tiny dot in the distance. As they got near the top, she saw the frozen lake appear, glittering in the early morning sun. And next to the lake were the Snow Cabins.

The other classes had said the Snow Cabins were awesome. Mira could see now that this wasn't an exaggeration. There was one big one in the middle and seven smaller ones around it, each one painted a different colour of the rainbow.

The children and their unicorns all got out of the cable car and began running over towards the cabins. The Art Bus was parked outside the

big cabin. Miss Hind was standing in the door and looking very warm with a hot chocolate.

'This is the teachers' cabin,' she said, waving at the big cabin behind her. 'The rainbow cabins are for you. Each class has its own colour.'

'It's going to be like sleeping in an igloo!' said Mira in delight, wanting a closer look at the red cabin where Class Red would be sleeping.

'Are they heated?' asked Darcy.

'Probably!' called Miss Glitterhorn from the hot tub outside the big teachers' cabin.

'Right, everyone!' said Miss Hind. 'Go and put your things in your cabin and then you can pick your winter morning activity.'

'Can we do sledging?' said Tom One.

'That is one of the activities,' said Miss Hind.

'YAAAAAAAAAAAAAAAY!' cheered all the children as they scattered towards their cabins.

Mira and the rest of Class Red raced through the snow to the red cabin. Mira threw her rucksack down on the nearest bed and pulled out the snack bag and poo shovel that she carried at all times when she was with Dave. She put them in her coat pockets as she walked back towards the teachers' cabin, kicking up snow with her snow boots. She couldn't wait for the activities to begin!

CHAPTER FOUR
Sledging and Snow Poos

When Mira walked past the yellow cabin she saw Rani and Lois outside with their unicorns. Rani was holding open the Beast Fighting Sack and they were both looking inside.

'I don't think we should leave ANY of the tools behind,' Rani was saying to Lois as Mira arrived. 'You can't be too careful with Snow Beasts.'

'But that sack looks so heavy,' said Mira.

'It will weigh down your sledge.'

Rani hissed at Mira in annoyance, but Lois said, 'She's got a point about the sledging. Maybe we could take just five tools to defeat the top five scariest Snow Beasts?'

Rani bit her lip and thought. 'Okay,' she agreed. 'So, number three is definitely yetis.'

Lois nodded. 'And number two is big yetis.'

'Yes,' said Rani. 'And number one is . . .'

'. . . the Abominable Snowman,' they said together.

Mira wanted to ask again why yetis were so scary, but she didn't get a chance, because Raheem and Brave had appeared and Raheem was asking if she thought Icicle Studies would be one of the activity options again.

Rani and Lois couldn't agree over which was scarier out of the Fanged Snow Sheep and the Poison Snow Gerbil for four and five, so in the end they just took all the Snow Beast Fighting Tools. Then they all quickly made their way

to the teachers' cabin where the teachers were already starting to announce the activities.

'Now for anyone who wants to do

sledging,' said Miss Glitterhorn, 'the sledges are all piled up at the side of the cabin. And –'

All the children and unicorns started running towards the pile of sledges.

'Don't you want to find out about the other activities?' said Miss Hind.

'We just want to sledge!' called Tom Two.

Miss Hind shrugged. Miss Glitterhorn hopped back into the hot tub.

'Are you going to come sledging, Miss Ponytail?' said Tamsin.

'Oh no,' said the art teacher, who was setting up some tables next to the Art Bus. 'It looks very steep and chilly. I am going to make sure everything is ready for the Aurora Lights later!'

She started laying out the art supplies on the tables.

Mira thought the art project would be fun, and she was really looking forward to seeing the Aurora Lights. But right now she couldn't wait to go sledging! She picked up an awesome-looking purple sledge.

'Come on, Dave!' she said, encouraging her UBFF with a few strawberry laces from the snack bag.

Dave gave a happy snort and trotted through the snow after Mira. They joined Darcy, Star, Raheem and Brave, who were all following the other children and their unicorns to the top of the sledging slope. Raheem said he'd decided to hunt for icicles and do sledging at the same time.

Soon Mira reached the top of the slope. Both the Toms had already set off and were whizzing down the slope with their unicorns. Darcy played some dramatic music on her phone as she and Star launched themselves forward on their gold sparkly sledge and started speeding down the hill. Rani's bright yellow sledge, on the other hand, kept stopping, as it was so weighed down by the sack of tools.

Mira dropped her sledge down into the snow and wiggled it so it was pointing down the slope. She sat in front of Dave. Mira knew that her unicorn might take this opportunity to do one of his extra-long super-farts and she didn't

want to be in the danger zone. She felt a tingly
mixture of nerves and excitement in her tummy
as she nudged the sledge forward . . . and they
were off!

They started sliding, going over little bumps
and picking up speed. Soon they were going
so fast that all the other children and unicorns
were a blur and ice spray was flying up around
them. It was So. Much. Fun. The only sound
louder than the whooshing of the sledge was
Dave's extra-long super-fart echoing round the
mountains. At one point they went over a bigger
bump and the sledge lifted up in the air for just
a second and Mira's tummy did a flip.

As soon as they got to the bottom, they raced

back up to the top to go again. Well, Mira raced

back up while Dave tried to have a nap on the

sledge. So Mira dropped a trail of biscuits

behind her and Dave soon got off the

sledge and followed on his four

short legs.

Mira could hear all the whoops of the other children as they whizzed past. Darcy announced she had retired from sledge hockey and was now a champion sledger instead. She, Tom One and Tom Two were weaving their sledges in and out of a course they'd made with their coats and hats. Miss Ponytail had warned that they would get too cold, but they'd told her they were 'having too much fun to be cold'.

Mira and Dave went down the slope five times. Tom One showed Mira how to make the sledge change direction using a technique called bum wiggling. So Mira and Dave gave that a go too, once Mira had bribed Dave with more biscuits. It wasn't easy, and they nearly ran over Raheem, but eventually they were able to swerve the sledge wonkily from side to side.

'Great bum wiggling, Dave!' said Mira, giving her UBFF a big hug as they were about to set off for their sixth trip down the slope.

Dave snorted in response. Then he hopped off, squatted down and did a giant poo right in front of the sledge. As his poos often were in cold weather, it was frosty and perfectly round, like a snowball.

Mira fumbled in her coat pocket for the poo shovel. Dave sat down behind her on the waiting sledge as it balanced at the top of the slope.

At that moment Darcy and Star came scooting past.

'Oh no!' said Darcy. 'Are you having trouble getting going?'

Darcy gave Mira a helpful shove and the sledge started to move. Mira turned around, thinking she'd need to shovel the poo when they came back up. And then she saw Raheem pointing to the front of her sledge.

They were pushing the poo along in front of them!

Mira and Dave whizzed down the slope, getting faster and faster and sending up ice spray, just like before. The poo rolled ahead of them through the snow, getting bigger and rounder.

All the children making their way back up the hill were stopping and pointing.

By now the poo had become so big that Mira could barely see over it. They were approaching the bottom of the slope, but they didn't seem to be slowing down . . . She hoped that they wouldn't roll into anyone!

'WHAT is THAT?' came Miss Hind's voice.

'It's the Abominable Snow Poo!' yelled Lois.

Mira peeped around the side of the rolling snow poo-ball to see Miss Hind and the other teachers getting closer and closer.

'Quick Dave!' she yelled, turning round. 'BUM WIGGLE!'

The little unicorn squeezed his eyes shut and did the biggest bum wiggle yet. The sledge swerved to the side, swooshing past the teachers and showering them with ice spray.

'Phew!' said Mira.

The giant snow poo rolled to the other side, also missing the teachers, and crashed into the art-supplies table.

CHAPTER FIVE
Snowy Surprise

Mira put the last of the felt tips in the pen pot and brushed the snow off the coloured card. It hadn't taken too long to set up the art table again and Dave had even been helping because Miss Hind said they couldn't have lunch until it was tidy.

It had taken three unicorns to move the giant snow poo-ball. No one was quite sure what to do with it, so they propped it up around the back of the teachers' cabin.

After lunch, Dave had a happy food nap and everyone else gathered around the newly tidied art table for Miss Ponytail to tell them about the art project. Darcy, Tom One and Tom Two tried to sneak off to go sledging again but Miss Hind dragged them back.

'What causes the Aurora Lights?' Freya asked.

'It's when the rainbows hug each other,' said Miss Ponytail.

'And because of Science,' said Miss Glitterhorn.

'Yes,' said Miss Ponytail brightly. 'Now it's time to choose your weapons!'

'Do you have nerf guns?' said Darcy hopefully as they approached the table.

'We have super-cool crayons and glitter glue!' said Miss Ponytail. 'It's important that you have plenty of art supplies with you so you can really capture the moment when it happens. Last time I was so overwhelmed by the wonder of it all that I dropped my pen in the snow and then I had to draw it all in my mind, so now I carry six pens at all times, just in case.'

Miss Ponytail had brought them all rainbow tote bags to put their art supplies in, which Mira thought was really nice of her. Mira picked some bright yellow card, purple glitter glue and neon green glow-in-the-dark paint and put it in her bag.

After the pipe cleaners had been shared out, there had been two fights over the rainbow crepe paper and Dave had eaten an entire tub of dried pasta, the tables were empty and everyone's tote bag was full. Rani had taken the opportunity to put some Snow Beast Fighting Tools in hers. This meant she could put the sack back in the cabin, but also that the only art supplies she had room for were a small pencil and a Post-it note.

Then Miss Ponytail pointed up, just to the side of the sledging hill. 'That is where the Aurora Lights will appear in the sky,' she said. 'Just a couple of hours to go now!'

It was time for the afternoon activities. Everyone picked sledging again, so soon they were all heading back up to the top of the slope on their unicorns. Mira sat on Brave with Raheem and they pulled Dave along on the sledge because he was still asleep.

Once they were at the top, Rani said that she wanted to bagsy the best place to watch the lights from later. Mira thought that sounded like a good idea, so she and Raheem started looking around too, trying to remember where Miss Ponytail had pointed in the sky.

'Save a spot for meeeeeeeeeeeeee,' called Darcy as she and Star started sledging down the slope backwards.

Rani had found a log. Once she'd checked it for Snow Beasts and declared it safe, she put her coat on it to claim it. But Mira was sure there was a better spot. There were quite a few tall trees around. What if they blocked the view?

Mira suddenly saw another hill through a break in the trees. 'Wait!' she said. 'That looks like an even better place to watch the lights . . .'

'And an EVEN better slope for sledging!' said Darcy, who had appeared next to her. 'It's got jumps and everything.'

Darcy and Star started scooting their sledge over to the left of the hill and Mira followed.

'We can't go down there,' Rani called after her. 'That's where the yetis are.'

'How do you know?' said Darcy, stopping and looking back.

'I've just got a feeling,' said Rani wisely.

Mira peered down the slope. 'It does look really good for sledging,' she said.

Rani rolled her eyes. 'You want to go there?' she said, rifling through her bag. 'We're gonna need some Snow Beast Fighting Tools.'

'We need these hats for definite,' said Lois, fishing some felt hats out of her own tote bag.

'Let's go down there and see if your tools really work!' cried Darcy.

Rani scoffed. 'They *do* work. We protected you from a Vicious Snow Gremlin just a few minutes ago.'

'I didn't see a Vicious Snow Gremlin,' said Darcy as Raheem looked around nervously.

'That's because we were so quick to act and we scared it off before you saw it,' said Rani.

'I think we should stick to the main slope,' said Raheem. 'Plus, there are some brilliant icicles in these trees I want to look at.'

Mira really wanted to go and explore the other slope, but she thought Raheem was probably right.

Darcy sighed. 'Fine,' she said as she and Star scooted back along the snow next to Mira. 'I don't want any yetis getting in the way of my sledge tricks anyway.'

'So, why are the yetis so scary?' Mira asked

Lois and Rani.

'They're huge,' said Lois. 'And furry. And they are completely ravenous. They eat and eat but are never satisfied.'

'They have stomachless bottoms,' said Rani.

'Do you mean bottomless stomachs?' said Raheem.

'They have the most gigantic feasts ever seen,' said Lois.

'It's just that everyone has stomachless bottoms,' said Raheem. 'Because no one has a stomach in their bottom.'

'At their feasts they eat unicorns for starters, adults for mains,' said Rani. 'And for dessert they eat . . .'

'CHILDREN!' Rani and Lois said together.

There was a silence and they all looked at each other. Even though it was already cold, Mira felt a chill.

'Let's not go where the yetis are,' she said.

'Okay but Dave already has,' said Darcy.

Mira spun around to see her UBFF scooting along on a purple sledge and disappearing over the crest of the other slope.

CHAPTER SIX
Where the YETIS are!

'WEEEEEEEEEEEEEEEEEEEEEEEEEEE
EEEEEEEE!' yelled Mira as she zoomed down
the slope.

Darcy had been right – this *was* the best slope
for sledging. Mira was sharing Raheem's sledge
while Brave was sliding down on his hooves.
They slid over big bumps in the snow where
they'd fly up into the air, which reminded Mira
of the time she went on the log flume at the
theme park with a really big drop and her dad

screamed so much another family complained.

Alongside them, Darcy and the Toms were doing tricks. On one of the jumps Darcy even did a somersault. Behind them were Rani and Lois and their unicorns, as Rani had said Mira and her friends would be useless at fighting the yetis without them. They were holding on to their felt hats to stop them flying off.

As they got nearer to the bottom of the slope, Mira could see Dave sitting on the purple sledge. Just then, they went over the biggest bump yet. The sledge sailed into the air. Mira and Raheem both fell off and came to a soft landing in the snow. As the others went over the big jump the same thing happened, and they all ended up in a heap.

Mira climbed to her feet, brushed the snow off her coat and ran over to Dave.

'Don't sledge off without me again,' she said. 'Even if it is to go down the best sledging slope ever.'

Dave gave a sorrowful fart and then nuzzled Mira's hand. Mira gave him a scratch behind the ears. She could never stay mad at her unicorn for long. Plus the sledging *had* been really fun.

She looked around and saw that they were in a big valley. The others were all getting to their feet and looking around too. It was very quiet, apart from the sound of the rest of the school sledging on the other slope.

'HELLO?' yelled Darcy. 'YETIS?'

Her voice echoed round and round the valley.
Then there was silence again.

'I don't think there are any yetis here,' said
Darcy.

'They must have seen our hats,' said Rani.
'Anyway, we'd better get back to the top.'

The others agreed and started climbing on
to their unicorns.

There was a strange rumbling sound.

'Does your unicorn ever stop farting?' said Rani, rolling her eyes at Mira.

'That's not Dave,' said Mira, frowning. She was an expert at recognising Dave's farts now, and could even tell what mood he was in from the sound. His mood was always either hungry or sleepy, but it was still a skill she was proud of.

The strange noise came again.

'It's kind of like a roar?' said Raheem. 'And . . . footsteps . . .'

Mira felt the ground vibrating under her feet. She looked at Raheem, whose eyes were wide. Slowly they started to turn around, just as a huge shadow fell over them . . .

'ROAAAAAAAR!'

roared the shadow.

'YETI YETI YETI!'

yelled Mira and Raheem.

Tom One and Tom Two held up

their sledges as shields. Dave jumped

into Mira's arms. Lois threw her felt hat at

them all and started running back

through the snow, yelling,

'SAVE YOURSELVES!'

'Guys,' said Darcy. 'The yeti's really small.'

Mira peeped over Dave. The yeti *was* small.

It was a bit like an overgrown teddy bear. It

stepped forward and picked up the felt hat,

sniffed it and ate it. Then the yeti jumped up and

down and waved.

Slowly, they all waved back.

'Remember, it's a Scary Snow Beast . . .' said

Rani, backing away.

The yeti lay down and did a snow angel.

'Well, we'd better get going,' said Rani. 'Bye, scary yeti.'

Mira waved at the yeti again.

'It was nice to meet you!' said Raheem.

The yeti stared at them all and then sat down on the snow with a *THUMP*. It threw back its head and started to howl.

'Is it . . . crying?' said Lois.

The little yeti looked really sad.

'Do you think it's lonely?' asked Mira.

'Or HUNGRY?' said Rani, her eyes narrowing suspiciously.

Dave burped loudly, as if to remind them that he was hungry too.

The yeti stopped howling and sniffed.

Then it also did a big burp. Dave burped back. Then they had a farting competition.

'Gross,' said Rani.

'My money's on Dave,' said Darcy.

'Hmm, I feel like the yeti could pull a ripper out of the bag,' said Tom One.

The yeti was back up on its feet now. It looked over at Tom One and then it picked up some snow. It made a snowball and threw it at him.

Tom One laughed and made one himself and threw it back. It landed right on the yeti's head! The yeti blinked. They all looked at each other, and Mira held her breath.

'I *told* you!' said Rani.

The yeti threw back its head and roared again. The roar sounded somehow different this time.

'I think it's laughing!' said Raheem.

The yeti threw another snowball that hit

Tom Two on the ear. Tom Two laughed and threw one back. Soon more of them were joining in and it became a proper snowball fight. The only one not taking part was Rani. She was standing at a distance and holding up her sledge as a shield and waggling the felt hat at the yeti whenever it ran past her.

'We should get back,' Rani said. 'The teachers will be wondering where we are.'

'They can see us,' said Tom Two, pointing up to the top of the slope they'd come down.

Mira looked. Sure enough, there was Miss Hind, leaning against a tree and having a snack. She gave them a short wave and then looked away. Miss Hind must have thought that the yeti

was someone in a furry snow suit. Either that or
she just wasn't very concerned about yetis.

'Okay, but we still can't be long,' said Rani,
'because this is where the yetis are so it's still the
scariest place on earth.'

'I don't see anything scary down here,' said
Tom One, looking around.

'Apart from that giant mouth about to eat us,'
said Darcy.

'Oh yeah,' said Tom Two.

A huge hole gaped from the side of the
mountain, covered on all sides with what looked
like sharp teeth . . .

CHAPTER SEVEN
The Winter Wonderland

'Those aren't teeth, they're icicles!' said Raheem, rushing over to look at them. Mira didn't think she'd ever heard him sound so excited. 'It's an ice cave. Just like in an ordinary cave, the ones that hang from the top are called stalactites and the ones that grow from the bottom are called stalagmites!'

'I think they should be called stalacticicles and stalagmicicles!' said Mira.

She followed Raheem over, and Raheem gave her a high five. Then Mira peeped into the ice cave. It was actually more of a short tunnel, with something glittering at the other end. The little yeti had joined them and was looking excited, but not as excited as Raheem.

'Can we have a quick look inside?' Raheem said.

Rani rolled her eyes. 'A very quick look,' she said. 'Lois and I will stand guard here as we're the oldest and the most responsible.'

'Yeah,' said Lois, who had just finished drawing a giant bum in the snow.

Mira and the others crept forward into the icy cave mouth. They wove carefully in and out of

the icicles, trying not to dislodge any of them. Raheem said they had taken hundreds of years to form.

'Follow me, Dave,' said Mira, helping her unicorn to find his way through. The other unicorns were elegantly picking up their feet, and Raheem's unicorn, Brave, was even trotting. But Mira knew that Dave might need a bit of extra help.

'THIS IS AWESOME!' called Darcy, just ahead of Mira on Star's back.

'What is it? I want to see!' called Rani from the entrance.

'Me too!' shouted Lois.

Mira and Dave stepped around the last icicle.

'Phew!' said Mira. She couldn't believe they'd made it through without damaging any of the icicles! 'Well done, Dave!' she said, giving her UBFF a scratch behind the ears.

Dave looked up at her proudly and then squeezed his eyes shut. Mira knew what was coming . . .

Rani, Lois, Angelica and Popcorn skidded to a halt behind Dave.

'Danger zone!' called Mira, but it was too late. Dave farted with such force that Rani and Angelica were knocked off their feet and three icicles broke off.

'GROSS!' yelled Rani. Angelica whinnied crossly.

'The icicles!' said Raheem, sprinting forward.

Darcy and Tom One had already grabbed two

of the icicles and started a sword fight. Raheem

carefully picked up the third one.

'Quick we need to put it in an icicle tray,' he said.

'What's an icicle tray?' said Lois, but Raheem had already got a tray out of his bumbag and was laying the icicle inside.

'Wow!' said Tom Two, looking ahead – and Mira realised what Darcy had been calling awesome just before.

'It's an ice palace!' said Tom One.

'It's better than that,' said Darcy. 'It's a winter wonderland – with an adventure playground!'

Darcy was right. Mira gasped as she looked around. They were in a huge ice dome, with a small hole at the top where she could see the sky. The whole surface of the dome was covered in spidery snowflake patterns. And laid out in front of them were twisty vines of snow and ice, creating a giant maze of climbing frames, huge slides, yet another sledging slope and a mega-steep bobsleigh ice run.

The little yeti came running into the cave behind them, hopping easily through the icicles. It did a forward roll along the ground and ran over to an ice see-saw. Then it sat on one end and looked up at them expectantly.

'We HAVE to play here or I will literally die,' said Darcy dramatically.

'We can't,' said Rani. 'This is a yeti's lair!' She straightened her felt hat and glared at the little yeti. The yeti saluted back.

'Anyway,' Rani continued. 'We have to go back up to the others or we'll get into trouble. AND I bet someone steals my spot for watching the lights!'

Mira looked away from the winter wonderland and back to her sister. She wanted to stay and play more than anything. The little yeti had got so sad when they'd tried to leave before.

And then she had a thought. She could find lots more friends for the little yeti!

'We should go back,' she said.

'NOOOO!' protested Darcy and the Toms.

'Wait!' said Mira. 'We should go back and get EVERYONE! Then we can all play down here until it's time for the aurora lights and the yeti won't be lonely, AND we won't get into trouble!'

'You are an actual genius!' said Darcy.

The others agreed with the plan. They all turned round to leave.

The little yeti looked over at them from its see-saw with a sad expression. Mira thought it might start crying again. She tried to explain what they were doing by pointing and then doing a mime. The little yeti put its head on one side. Then it climbed off the see-saw and followed them out through the icicles.

'It's okay, we're coming back,' said Mira, as they walked back across the valley and towards the slope.

The yeti growled happily and bounded through the snow next to them.

'I guess it's coming with us!' said Mira.

∪∪∪

Everyone was on their unicorns as they climbed back up the hill, except Mira, who was on

Brave with Raheem again. The yeti was giving Dave a piggyback. Rani was frowning and checking her tote bag. Rani would

never admit it, but Mira could tell she was disappointed she hadn't needed to use any of the Beast Fighting Tools.

Soon they were up at the top of the hill again. All the other children were still sledging while Miss Hind supervised and Miss Ponytail was setting up her easel.

'Hey everyone!' yelled Mira, waving her arms. 'We have something AWESOME to tell you!'

Miss Hind frowned and Miss Ponytail looked up from her easel. Children who were walking up with their sledges stopped. A boy called Yusuf from Class Indigo was just positioning his sledge at the top of the slope close to Mira. His eyes widened and he pointed behind her.

'WHAT'S THAT?' he cried.

Mira turned back just as the yeti let out a thundering roar. Then it did a friendly wave.

'YETI YETI YETI!' yelled Yusuf, launching his sledge down the slope.

Everyone screamed and started running towards the cabins.

CHAPTER EIGHT
Frozen Friendships

When they reached the cabins Mira explained that the yeti wasn't scary. The yeti was doing cartwheels in the snow behind her and looking very cute, which helped. Eventually everyone came out to meet it and Flo from Mira's class gave it a big hug. Miss Glitterhorn gave them a wave from the hot tub, where she'd been since lunch time. Then Miss Hind sledged down the slope, casually slaloming from side to side and finishing off with a loop-the-loop.

'What's all this snow silliness?' she said.

The yeti stopped cartwheeling and stood still
with its furry hand on its mouth.

Mira told them all about meeting the yeti and
the winter wonderland, while Darcy and Lois
chipped in with details about the 'epic snowball
fight' and 'running into a monster's mouth'.

'It was a cave of icicles, not an actual monster's mouth!' said Raheem, when some of the children looked alarmed.

'Oh, that's a shame,' said Flo.

'The winter wonderland is basically the best place I've ever seen,' said Mira. 'And I thought that we could all go and play there with the yeti?'

All around her, everyone began squealing with excitement. Mira hopped up and down on the snow. She wanted to get back to the winter wonderland right away!

'Hmmm,' said Miss Hind, and raised her eyebrow.

Mira stopped hopping.

'You want to go and play with a yeti inside a monster's mouth, on items made entirely from ice?' said Miss Hind.

Mira's heart began to sink. She'd imagined coming back here and everyone immediately racing off to the winter wonderland (possibly while cheering her name). She hadn't thought the teachers might say no! She had to think quickly . . .

'I just thought it would be a very good opportunity for Icicle Studies,' Mira said.

'It really would!' said Raheem.

Mira looked up at Miss Hind and held her breath.

'Well,' said Miss Hind. 'I find it encouraging

that you would like to do something other than sledging.'

'The winter wonderland has a big indoor sledging slope,' said Tom Two.

'And an ice-skate park!' said Darcy.

All the children cheered.

'I'm still thinking!' said Miss Hind loudly and they started whisper-cheering instead.

'Please please please!' chorused Tamsin and Seb.

Miss Hind looked at them all. Then she looked at the yeti. It still had its hand on its mouth and was looking up at her with pleading eyes.

'As the yeti seems to be the most well behaved of all of you, I will allow this as a special

activity,' said the teacher.
The cheer that went
around was louder than a
yeti's roar. Miss Hind told
them to be quiet before she
changed her mind.

They all scrambled back
up the slope and found
Miss Ponytail. She'd
hidden up a tree when
the yeti had appeared
and was having trouble
getting down. Once a
few of the unicorns had
helped her, Mira and

Darcy told her about the winter wonderland.

'That does sound lovely,' Miss Ponytail said.
'We must be quick, though, or we'll miss the
lights.' They reassured her that they would be
quick – and Rani made sure that no one had
taken her spot with the best view of the lights.

'You'll really like it, Miss,' said Tom Two.
'We think it's going to be the best sledging yet!'

'Oh, I'm not really a fan of sledging,' said
Miss Ponytail.

Up ahead, Tom One's unicorn, Blazing
Saddle, stopped.

'But Miss,' said Tom One, 'everyone loves
sledging!'

Miss Ponytail shrugged. 'Anyway, don't forget

your art-supply bags! We'll have to go straight from the winter wonderland to the top of the slope to see the Aurora Lights and paint them for our special art project!'

The whole school and their unicorns grabbed their art supplies. Then they followed Mira and her friends to the winter wonderland, with Mira, the little yeti and Dave in the lead. They went down the awesome sledging slope, across the valley and through the cave of icicles. Mira, Darcy, the Toms, Lois, Rani and their unicorns showed the others how to weave their way inside. And when Dave made his way successfully through for the second time that day, and for the second time prepared to do a proud fart, Mira quickly swivelled him round so his bum was pointing away from the icicles.

Unfortunately, his bum was then pointing towards Rani and the blast knocked her over again. She angrily chased Mira around the ice roundabout.

Everyone agreed that the winter wonderland was indeed the most awesome place on earth.

'I'm going to go on the snow swing!' said Tanya from Class Green.

'Thanks for bringing us here, Mira!' said Jimmy, who was also from Class Green.

Mira was still being chased by Rani, but she looked over her shoulder. 'It's okay! But it was really all of us who found —'

Mira trailed off and Rani stopped running.
A big shadow had fallen over them . . .

Underneath Mira's feet, the ground was
vibrating.

A huge furry creature came stomping into the
winter wonderland. It looked just like the little
yeti, but was at least five times the size.

'YETI YETI YETI!' shouted Yusuf.

'That's not just a yeti . . .' said Lois.

'IT'S THE ABOMINABLE SNOWMAN!'

yelled Rani.

Around them the children scattered and
hid behind different bits of the ice adventure
playground. Miss Ponytail dived underneath
the ice slide.

The yeti was holding something in its giant hairy paws. It looked like some bits of a hedge. It ran in a circle, waving the twigs and leaves around. Mira thought it looked scared, which was odd . . .

Rani pulled out her felt hat. Lois didn't have her felt hat any more because the little yeti had eaten it, so the two of them tried to stretch Rani's hat over both their heads.

The big yeti stared at Rani and Lois and let out an earth-shattering yelp. Its footsteps made the ground shake as it ran and hid behind a tiny ice swing with its paws over its eyes.

There was silence, apart from the fading echoes of the big yeti's yelps.

The little yeti sighed. It ran over to the swing where the big yeti had gone. A few moments later it reappeared, dragging the big yeti by its white furry paw. The big yeti looked nervously at them all.

'I think yetis are as scared of us as we are of them!' said Mira.

'And they have tools too!' said Lois.

She pointed at the yeti's other paw, which was clutching the hedge bits. The big yeti was still staring warily at Lois and Rani's hat. Rani and Lois quickly took it off and put it in Lois's bag. The big yeti gave a tiny smile and lowered its twigs and leaves.

Then they all played in the ice adventure

playground. Darcy announced she had retired from sledging and taken up bobsleighing. Children and unicorns climbed all over the twisty vines of ice and swung across the frozen monkey bars. Raheem, Seb, Tamsin, their unicorns and the little yeti built a snow yeti right in the middle of the winter wonderland. Then the big yeti lifted Raheem up so he could pop the broken-off icicle on the snow yeti's head.

'It's the Abominable Snowmanicorn!' said Raheem, and everybody whooped.

Unfortunately, the big yeti whooped too and threw its arms up, so Raheem went flying through the air and landed in a freshly made pile of snowballs.

The little yeti was skipping around. It looked
like it was having the best time, and it wanted
to play with everyone! Mira's favourite bit
was when the little yeti came over to the ice
roundabout and she and Rani showed it 'Epic
Roundabout Hurricane Spin' which was a game
they played in the local playground at home.

No one could spin a roundabout as fast as Rani!

Miss Hind had joined Darcy on the mega-steep bobsleigh ice track, but Mira couldn't see Miss Ponytail anywhere. And then she heard her.

'WEEEEEEEEEEEEEEEEEEE!' yelled Miss Ponytail, sledging down the indoor sledging slope.

'See, everyone loves sledging!' said Tom One.

They carried on playing different games for ages. It was getting darker and darker, and getting a bit difficult to see. But as soon as Mira thought that, a collection of icy orbs dotted around the sides of the dome flickered and began to glow.

'That is epic!' said Tom Two and Mira nodded. But then she had a thought.

'If it's dark . . .' she said. 'WE MISSED THE AURORA LIGHTS!'

CHAPTER NINE
Lights Out?

Mira looked around in panic.

'We have to get back for the Aurora Lights!' she said, turning to Raheem. 'Do you think we can make it in time to see them and do our special art project?'

Mira and Raheem frantically started gathering up their art-supply bags. Mira couldn't believe they'd lost track of time so much! What was Miss Ponytail going to say?

'Miss Ponytail!' she gasped. 'The Aurora Lights!'

There was a swoosh of snow spray as the art teacher sledged over.

'It's okay, Mira,' said Miss Ponytail. 'It was a lovely idea to bring everyone to play with the yeti. And they're all having so much fun – they won't want to leave. I think we'll have to miss the Aurora Lights this year.'

'There's always the next ones in seventy million years,' said Sarah from Class Blue.

'And sledging *is* actually quite fun,' said Miss Ponytail. She smiled and headed up the slope with her sledge again, but Mira thought she looked a bit sad. She wished they had gone to the winter wonderland AND seen the Aurora Lights.

'Maybe we can see a bit of them from the valley,' Mira said.

A spark of light suddenly glimmered on the snow next to her. Mira turned to look, but it disappeared. Then she glimpsed another spark out of the corner of her eye.

'Did you see that, Dave?' she said.

But when she turned to look at her UBFF . . .

Dave was rainbow-coloured!

'Dave! Are you okay? Is it something you've eaten?' Mira said, feeling alarmed. 'Hey guys! I think Dave ate a rainbow!'

'No, look!' said Raheem.

Mira turned to see what Raheem was
pointing at. The icicle in the middle of the
Abominable Snowmanicorn's head looked like
it was glowing. The rainbows from the Aurora
Lights were shining in through the small hole
in the ice cave roof. And
then the light rays
were bouncing
off the icicle
and shining
all around the
ice adventure
playground. It
looked like the
rainbows were

jumping and shimmering all around them.

'QUICK! CAPTURE THE MOMENT!'
yelled Miss Ponytail, leaping off her sledge and
ripping open her art-supplies bag to get at her
paints.

Everyone ran over to their bags and grabbed
their art supplies. Then they all sat in the winter
wonderland, sketching, painting, sculpting and –
in Flo's case – slime-making.

Seb mixed the glow-in-the-dark paints to

make a painting that shimmered just like the
icicle.

'I drew mine in snow!' said Tamsin, holding
up a completely blank piece of paper.

Darcy quickly took a picture on her phone
and carried on sledging.

Mira and Dave sat next to the little yeti to do
their drawing. After sketching the rainbows,
Mira decided to add her, Dave and the little yeti
having a snowball fight. When she'd finished,

she showed the drawing to the yeti, who gave Mira a big hug. Mira wondered if the yeti would enjoy drawing. She gave it a piece of paper and some colouring pencils, but the yeti just looked at them and then ate them.

Miss Ponytail was walking around and looking at the different art projects. She was particularly impressed with Miss Hind's watercolour snowscape in the style of Monet.

Then she got to Rani and Lois, who were sitting empty-handed.

Oh no! thought Mira. She remembered how Rani and Lois hadn't had much room in their bags for art materials . . .

'What did you make?' said Miss Ponytail.

Rani pointed. Beside her and Lois was a sculpture of feathers, felt, an empty honey jar and lots of other objects.

They'd made art out of ALL their Snow Beast Fighting Tools!

CHAPTER TEN

Back to Unicorn School

The next morning Mira woke up early. Mainly because Miss Ponytail and Miss Hind had said the little yeti could have a sleepover in the Class Red cabin, and it took up quite a lot of the bed.

The teachers had said they would have more trips to visit the yeti again, and the yetis could also come and visit the school now everyone knew they weren't scary. But Mira was still feeling sad about leaving the little yeti. She looked at her drawing of them all having so much fun with the Aurora Lights all around them. It was a memory she knew she would never forget.

'Hey, Mira!' whispered Raheem from the bunk below. 'Are you awake?'

'Yes!' whispered Mira, popping her head over the bunk bed.

'I've had an idea,' Raheem whispered. 'A nice surprise we could do for the yeti.'

He explained what his idea was.

'That's brilliant, Raheem!' Mira whispered, a bit louder than she'd meant to. The little yeti snored and Dave sleep-farted.

Mira and Raheem crept around the cabin,

waking up the rest of Class Red and telling them Raheem's plan. They all thought it was brilliant too! A few of them went to the other cabins to pass it on. Mira went to see Miss Hind and Miss Ponytail. After initially being grumpy at being woken up so early, the teachers both agreed that it was a very nice idea.

And so, leaving a few people at the Class Red cabin in case the yeti woke up, they made their way back over to the winter wonderland.

∪∪∪

By the time they'd all crept back into the cabins, it was actually time to get up. The yeti seemed very excited to eat breakfast and had seconds, thirds, fourths and fifths of porridge.

124

Mira thought that Lois and Rani were right about the yetis having bottomless stomachs, even though they'd luckily been wrong about them eating children and unicorns. Most of all, she couldn't wait for the yeti to see the surprise they'd prepared!

Once breakfast was finished and they'd packed
up their stuff, they all accompanied the little
yeti back to its winter wonderland home. It was
walking slowly and dragging its feet. Mira could
tell it was sad for them to leave as well.

They climbed the slope and walked past the
trees where they had planned on watching the
Aurora Lights. Mira and Dave were walking
alongside Rani and Lois. Rani didn't have her

Beast Fighting Sack any more. As well as using lots of the Beast Fighting Tools to make their art display, Rani and Lois had also given the beast flutes to the yetis, as it turned out that they were actually very talented flute players. And Dave had eaten all the weapons that were edible (and some that weren't).

Dave stopped walking and did another frozen snow poo, so Mira searched in her bag for the

poo shovel. But then there was a strange rustling sound.

Everyone else stopped too and looked around to see where the noise was coming from. Then some snow spiders came scuttling out of the trees! Raheem's unicorn Brave was very frightened of spiders, so he whinnied and leaped into a pile of snow to take shelter.

'What defeats snow spiders?' Tamsin asked Rani and Lois.

'We don't have the tools any more!' said Lois.

Rani ran forward. 'Quick, Lois! Throw me that poo!'

Lois dashed forward and grabbed Dave's frozen snow poo. She threw it to Rani, who kicked it towards the snow spiders, scattering them back into the trees.

All the classes cheered for Rani and Lois.

'You saved us from the Snow Beasts!' shouted the Toms.

'With a bit of help from the Abominable Snow Poo,' said Rani, grinning at Dave and Mira.

Mira grinned back at her sister. She was pleased that Rani had been able to use a Beast Fighting Tool. Even if it was a poo.

They all sledged down the best sledging slope one last time and they were nearly at the winter wonderland. The big yeti was waiting for them outside the ice cave and gave Mira and Raheem a furry thumbs-up. Then they all wove their way through the icicles and back into the big ice play dome.

The little yeti trudged at the back. But when it walked into the ice dome it looked up – and its eyes widened in surprise.

Everyone's pieces of art were displayed all over the walls, making a giant mural. The big yeti had helped them to hang some of them really high up. And right in the middle of the display there was a gap.

'Ready?' said Darcy, who was sitting with the Toms next to a projector.

'Three!' said Tom One.

'Two!' said Tom Two.

'One!' said Tom One.

'GO!' they said together and hit a button on the projector.

In the gap on the wall, photos began to appear.

They were all the pics that Darcy had taken on

her phone. There were pictures of them sledging,

having a snowball fight with the yeti and playing

in the ice adventure playground. But
the most beautiful one was the one Darcy
had taken of the Aurora Lights, with all the
rainbows dancing on the walls of the dome.

Everyone sat and watched the photos while the little yeti clapped its furry paws. Then it gave every single child and unicorn a hug.

The teachers said they could come back soon to visit the yetis – and that the yetis could come and visit Unicorn School too! And after lots of cheering and even more furry yeti hugs, all the classes were on the trek home to Unicorn School.

Everyone was talking about their own favourite part of the winter wonderland. Darcy, Tom One and Tom Two said the mega bobsleigh was the best. Freya and Seb couldn't decide between the twisty-turny ice slide and the climbing wall, and Raheem couldn't decide between the seventeen icicles in the monster-ish cave mouth. Tamsin said it was the moment all the rainbows shone on the wall of the icy dome and Flo said that now she'd hugged a yeti her life was complete.

'What do you think, Dave?' said Mira, giving her UBFF a squeeze as he trotted along. 'It was ALL so epic, I can't choose the best bit!'

Dave burped happily. Mira decided that when you were with your UBFF, everything became an adventure. She couldn't wait to see what would happen next!

Then she fell off Dave's back as Dave suddenly squatted down and did his biggest snow poo yet.

Mira smiled to herself as she rummaged in her bag for the poo shovel. She might not know

what their next adventure would be, but there was one thing she knew for sure – Dave would always be full of surprises.

And poos.

**Enjoy more snowy adventures
in The Naughtiest Unicorn
at Christmas!**

CHAPTER ONE
Snow Much Fun!

'Look, there's some snow!' cried Mira excitedly as she leapt out of the car in the leisure-centre car park.

Her sister Rani stepped out of the car and peered over, wrinkling her nose. 'That,' she said, 'is *slush.*'

Mira bent closer to the small pile of snow, which was a *bit* slushy. And grey. 'There's definitely some specks of white,' she said. She had been so excited when she looked out of the window the night before and saw snowflakes falling. Mira's mum and dad said it wouldn't settle, but Mira was *sure* that she could find some to play with. It was the week before Christmas, and she had spent *days* planning fun things to do, ALL of which involved snow.

'You couldn't even get a snowball out of that,' said Rani, as Mira reached towards the slushy puddle.

'Time to go!' said their mum quickly. 'You don't want to be late for Unicorn School.'

And Mum was right – Mira absolutely did not want to be late for Unicorn School! Unicorn School was the best thing ever. You were paired up with your UBFF (Unicorn Best Friend Forever) and you went on quests and magical adventures. And even the ordinary lessons were a million

UBFFs 4 EVER

per cent better than the ones at normal school because the unicorns were there!

Mira, Rani and Mum walked over to the corner of the car park, where the magic portal to Unicorn School lay hidden behind some bushes. There was a queue of children waiting for their turn to go through. Everyone was wearing brightly-coloured festive jumpers.

Christmas was Mira's *favourite* time of year. She loved seeing her breath in the chilly air, the way trees sparkled with frost and being cosy inside with a mug of hot chocolate. (She had a feeling that her greedy unicorn, Dave, would enjoy the hot chocolate too.)

Mira quickly looked through her school bag

to make sure that she had everything. There were LOTS of pairs of thick woolly socks (added by her mum), treats for Dave, her pencil case and something very important: *The Legend of the Snow Unicorn*.

Every year at Christmas time, Class Red performed a play of *The Legend of the Snow Unicorn* and before they went home at the end of the last visit their teacher, Miss Glitterhorn, had given them each a script to learn. Mira knew the whole thing off by heart and she was

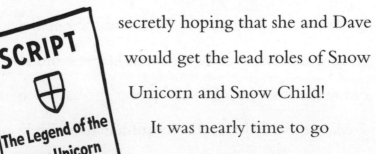

secretly hoping that she and Dave would get the lead roles of Snow Unicorn and Snow Child!

It was nearly time to go

through the portal and Rani said Mum had to
go where the other parents were all standing
huddled together, so Mum gave them each a hug
and a kiss and told them for about the eightieth
time to wrap up warm.

'Will there be snow at Unicorn School?'
Mira asked her sister.

'Only if you do the snow dance,' said Rani.

'What's the snow dance?' said Mira.

Rani sighed. 'It's quite difficult. Only Class
Yellow can do it. You probably won't manage it.'

Mira narrowed her eyes. She didn't always
believe the things her sister told her, but she also
didn't want to take any chances. Especially when
it came to unicorn stuff. Rani had been at school

for longer than Mira and had LOTS of medals, as she always liked to remind Mira.

'Just tell me how to do the snow dance,' she said.

'Fine!' said Rani. 'You have to squat like a frog and then stomp around, waving your hands in the air and grunting.'

Mira shuffled into position.

'Make sure you close your eyes and really get into it,' said Rani.

Mira started doing the snow dance. It was a bit slippy and slidey on the slushy floor, but the dance wasn't hard at all — she didn't know what Rani was on about.

'Mira . . .?'

Mira opened her eyes. Her friend Darcy

was there, looking concerned. Lots of the other

children were backing away.

'I'm doing the snow dance,' said Mira.

'Oh. I thought you just really needed the loo.'

WINTER WORDSEARCH

Can you find these ten words in the wordsearch? They could be hidden up, down, diagonally or backwards so look carefully!

SLEDGING	ICICLE
POO	PLAYGROUND
YETI	UNICORNS
AURORA	SACK
SNOW BEASTS	SNOW SPIDERS

I	Z	X	Y	T	L	L	T	Y	F	P	S
C	U	Q	K	W	Y	Q	Z	Y	B	T	R
I	N	Y	C	D	X	Y	Z	E	X	R	E
C	I	Y	A	Y	Z	M	Y	T	X	M	D
L	C	K	S	L	E	D	G	I	N	G	I
E	O	X	X	J	Z	W	Z	Y	M	Y	P
Q	R	Y	P	M	A	V	Q	X	P	Q	S
Z	N	B	P	R	Z	Q	Y	Y	V	Q	W
Z	S	N	O	W	B	E	A	S	T	S	O
V	V	R	O	Z	W	Q	Y	Y	J	Y	N
Q	U	Z	Q	W	T	Q	M	Z	K	Q	S
A	V	P	L	A	Y	G	R	O	U	N	D

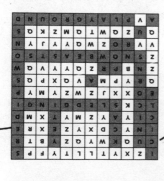

Catch up on ALL of Mira and Dave's Adventures at Unicorn School!

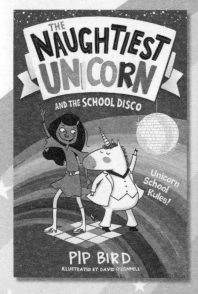

THE NAUGHTIEST UNICORN ON A SCHOOL TRIP

PIP BIRD

ILLUSTRATED BY DAVID O'CONNELL

THE NAUGHTIEST UNICORN ON THE BEACH

Fun in the sun!

PIP BIRD

ILLUSTRATED BY DAVID O'CONNELL

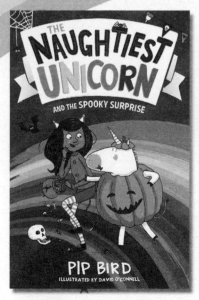

THE NAUGHTIEST UNICORN AND THE SPOOKY SURPRISE

PIP BIRD

ILLUSTRATED BY DAVID O'CONNELL

THE NAUGHTIEST UNICORN ON HOLIDAY

PIP BIRD

ILLUSTRATED BY DAVID O'CONNELL